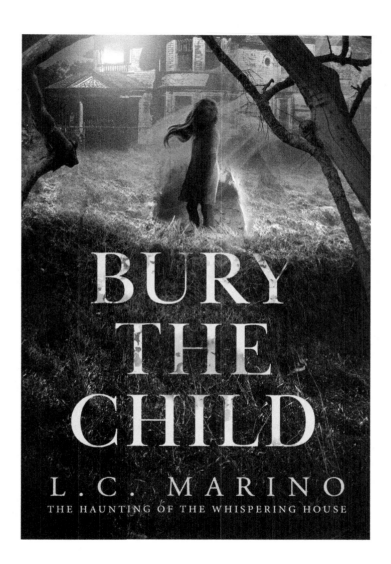

# BURY THE CHILD

## L.C. MARINO

### THE HAUNTING OF THE WHISPERING HOUSE

Paperback ISBN: 978-1-960535-07-8
Hardcover ISBN: 978-1-960535-08-5
eBook ISBN: 978-1-960535-06-1

# CONTENTS

# DEDICATION

This book is dedicated to the loving mothers of beloved children. This is a story of loss and grief so great it cannot be overcome. Yet, those emotions pale in comparison to the love which motivates you. The love of a mother for a child is the greatest power in the world.

I've experienced this love twice in my life. I feel that love as a son and I observe that love as a husband and father.

I love you, Mom.

I love you, Tammie.

# CHAPTER ONE
## AUGUST 16, 1966

The morning sun, so mercilessly bright, felt like an unwelcome intruder on this day of grief. It was as if the clouds had abandoned the sky after the early morning rainstorm, taking all the hope of the world with them as they fled.

It felt wrong for the sun to shine down over a child's funeral.

Lydia Jones, mother of the deceased Adeline and devoted wife of Wade, stood in a daze in the family cemetery sheltered by the woods behind their home. The remnants of that earlier morning's showers and the loose soil of her daughter's grave muddied her black leather shoes. Tears hung on Lydia's lashes and burned the swollen skin beneath her eyes.

She stared into the empty grave, the world around her muffled and raw. Overwhelming sorrow anchored her feet to the wet grass, preventing her from slowly pitching forward into the gaping earth before her.

Several men, eyes cast anywhere but at Lydia, approached the head of the grave, each bearing their share of the casket's weight with nine-year-old Adeline lying inside.

A tremor took hold of Lydia, her stomach twisting in knots that hadn't been there before. It wasn't the devastation she had grown accustomed to—it was something new, something fearful.

The pallbearers flanked each side of the grave, breathing in light fits as they steadied the casket above the hole and shifted the weight of their load from handle to rope. Hand over hand, they slowly lowered Adeline to her new home within the earth. Mere seconds later, the casket met the moist dirt floor below, relieving the men of their toil. Perfectly polished surfaces pressed into Virginia clay.

There, in the crude hole dug the day before by several men of the town, lay Lydia's entire world—her beloved daughter, Adeline.

A held breath slowly seeped out of Lydia. She felt her heart racing as her mind steadily wound under the coiling pressure of anxiety. She was at odds with herself. On the outside, she appeared stunned, breathless, and unmoving.

On the inside, a fire built as the fuel of fear, anger, and hopelessness flooded every corner of her mind.

Everything felt impossible. How could she bury her child, then simply walk away? It wasn't supposed to be like this. Adeline was supposed to bury Lydia, many years from now.

Lydia stood like a pillar; her feet felt cast in concrete. Beside her, Wade remained silent. She felt his heart breaking with hers. He was a good man. But the particular brand of despair, the one that only a mother burying her child could feel, was uniquely hers.

Father Pritchard's voice broke the silence. "Adeline now rests with our loving savior. May He watch over her, as she watches over us. She is now in His eternal light, His loving embrace, His protection. Never again shall she feel pain, only love. In Jesus' name, amen."

Lydia lifted her eyes to the small group of mourners surrounding the site. Several leaned on each other in their grief. Hunched shoulders, downcast eyes, and the occasional sniffle painted a genuine portrait of communal sorrow. And rightfully so—burying a child is uniquely dispiriting.

Father Pritchard gathered a handful of loose dirt from the digger's pile. He walked to Lydia, prepared to guide her through the conclusion of the ceremony.

His voice reverberated through her, "Ashes to ashes, dust to dust. May Adeline return to the soil we own."

Father Pritchard tossed the handful of dirt onto the lid of the coffin, and an unraveling began deep within Lydia. Soon, her child would rest beneath a mound of dirt, void of light and warmth.

She would never again see Adeline. She would never touch her or hold her. See her smile. Grow into a woman. Lydia would never get to hold Adeline's own child.

How long would it take for Lydia to forget the details of Adeline's face? Would she see her clearly in her dreams? Would her voice remain in Lydia's mind? Or would she lose that over time?

As she asked these questions and pondered her new reality, an overwhelming wave of loss broke over Lydia. She felt Wade's hands on her shoulders as he gently turned her away from the grave and toward their house. She could not think, could not speak. Lydia glanced over her shoulder as the single file procession made its way down the path to her home.

The last thing she saw over the bobbing line of mourners in her wake was a pallbearer pitching a shovel load of dirt onto the child below.

# CHAPTER TWO

Lydia's new life began the day after Adeline's funeral. She woke that morning with sore eyes and throat, the remnants of another night of poor sleep and unrelenting tears. The world seemed to move around Lydia in a monotonous blur, every action, every breath, devoid of purpose or sensation.

She started her day as best she could, avoiding direct contact with Wade as he quietly set about his morning routine. Lydia felt guilty, knowing Wade was going through this same thing with her, but she didn't have the stomach for conversation.

The atmosphere of the house felt stagnant and deafeningly silent. *I can do this*, Lydia thought as she floated through the first floor to the sunlit kitchen. Wade had beaten her to the kitchen and stood before a freshly brewed pot of coffee. She moved to the counter to prepare her usual breakfast of a hard-boiled egg and a few slices of toast. As Lydia went through the paces, she reflected fondly on how her best friend Sara had been so supportive over the past week. She'd stayed by her side like a shadow as Lydia and Wade handled the morbid task of planning Adeline's funeral.

Lydia had tried and failed several times to write Adeline's obituary. Sara had found her sobbing quietly at the desk in Adeline's room, the draft obituary catching her tears. "Let me help you, dear," Sara had said, guiding Lydia slowly from her chair to the darkness of the primary bedroom down the hall, where Lydia had cried herself to sleep yet again. When Lydia awoke, Sara was gone, having left to submit the obituary to the *Colonial Courier* before they closed their office for the evening.

Sara had also stood with her arm intertwined in Lydia's as she chose the child's ultimate resting place in the family cemetery behind the home. Later that day, Lydia had leaned into Sara as she selected her daughter's casket at Gracey Funeral Home.

Images of Sara, tirelessly at her side, gnawed at the corners of Lydia's conscience. Lydia felt a tinge of guilt from the burden she'd inadvertently put on Sara. *What kind of best friend makes you plan her child's funeral?* Lydia's guilt deepened. Adeline had been close to Sara. In the daze of the funeral preparations, Lydia hadn't given a moment's consideration to the anguish Sara must have experienced.

Overwhelmed with concern and on the verge of tears yet again, Lydia felt the immediate need to call Sara. Her guilt overtook her desire to avoid conversation, and she quickly turned from the counter toward the phone hanging on the wall and ran directly into Wade. The coffee in his hand sloshed from the cup, seeping into his shirt and pants.

"Whoa!" Wade exclaimed, jumping back to avoid any further contact with Lydia. Coffee ran down his hand to the kitchen floor. His face was flush, frustration clearly held behind pursed lips.

Lydia shook her head, eyes taking in the mess's totality as she muttered an apology that neither of them understood.

The words spilled from her in a torrent, "I'm so sorry. I was just thinking. The phone is on that wall, and I needed to call Sara. I didn't even hear you come into the room, let alone pour your coffee. I—"

"Well, isn't that a surprise," Wade said, cutting her off. "You were thinking about Sara again."

Immediate regret spread across his face as the coffee pooled around his feet.

His words felt like he'd tossed a bucket of ice water onto her face.

"What is *that* supposed to mean?" she asked in a slightly more defensive tone than she intended.

"Nothing. I didn't mean it. Let's just get this cleaned up." He sighed, quickly moving past his blunder.

He reached for the dishtowel hanging from the handle in front of the sink. Lydia stopped him by gently grabbing his wrist. Of course, Wade would choose one of her good dishtowels rather than one of the old rags from under the sink.

"No, what did you mean?" Lydia's emotions quickly moved from apologetic to agitated.

Wade closed his eyes for a moment, clearly assembling a response in his head. Lydia saw his hesitation as an honest attempt to avoid a poorly timed argument. They were on edge and wounded, having buried their daughter just twenty-four hours ago.

"I'm sorry, Lydia. I know Sara was very helpful to you last week. I didn't mean to sound upset. Let's just—"

"*Us.* Sara was very helpful to *us* last week. I feel guilty that I put so much on her. Maybe if you had been a bit more helpful, we wouldn't be having this conversation."

Wade pushed back. "I tried to be more helpful, but every time I turned around, Sara was glued to your side. I wanted to do more, but you wouldn't let me. I'm sorry, but I didn't want to start a fight as we planned our daughter's funeral."

His words hung like poison gas in the air between them.

Lydia stood like a stone pillar, her eyes closed and hands shaking. "I can't do this right now."

She turned, head down, and hurried to the back door. She fled through the back porch and into the yard before Wade could stop her.

Lydia stood in the humid Virginia air, the earth shedding moisture to the relenting summer sun. She held her hands over her face as she wept, the guilt she'd felt earlier now shared between Sara and Wade. Wade was right; Lydia had inadvertently pushed him away while they stumbled through Adeline's funeral plans. She hadn't really considered Wade at all the last week. What a terrible thing for a wife to know about herself. The ever-present pain of her loss compounded with the realization that she was hurting the man she loved.

Lydia turned and opened her eyes. She quieted as she squinted against the harsh sunlight pouring over the treetops. The path to the family plot behind the trees unfolded before her.

Lydia stopped crying, wiping the tears from her cheeks as something within her hardened. A strange, dark voice spoke up within her mind.

*No one feels bad for you. Life's tough. Just ask your dead daughter. Learn your lessons and move on, Lydia.*

The sun ducked behind a group of encroaching clouds. The yard before her grew darker, and a distant bout of thunder sent a warning to those in its path.

Lydia quieted like a scolded child. She sniffled and looked away from the path as quickly as she could. Something felt—off.

Fleeing to the yard had been a mistake. This place wasn't the sanctuary it had once been.

A slow surge of panic crept within Lydia's chest. She turned her face to the sky and closed her eyes as the sun emerged from the other side of the clouds. Her vision burst into a kaleidoscope of oranges and reds beneath her illuminated eyelids.

Lydia stood there for what felt like forever, breathing slowly and deliberately.

*I'm going to be okay. I just need to breathe.*

The racing thoughts in her mind slowed as she concentrated on her breathing.

A few minutes later, she lowered her head and opened her eyes. Everything looked filtered through a brightened screen as her eyes adjusted to the morning light. Lydia stole one quick glance at the path winding out of view into the woods before turning back toward the house.

She wiped her face and straightened her clothes as she traversed the yard, ascended the back steps, and entered the screened-in porch.

She stepped into the quiet house, carefully closing the door behind her. A moment later, she heard Wade's feet above her, upstairs. She looked about the kitchen to assess the job ahead. Thankfully, Wade had cleaned the mess from the kitchen floor, leaving no trace of the morning's confrontation.

*That will be one more notch on the guilt belt, ma'am. Please and thank you.*

Lydia took a seat at the kitchen table to gather her thoughts. Her eyes anxiously crawled the room before pausing momentarily. There, on the counter, where it had been for damn near ten years, was the small basket Lydia and Wade used to unclutter the kitchen counter. Wedged amongst their keys, loose batteries, pens, and other clutter was a worn deck of playing cards.

Lydia's shoulders dropped slowly under the weight of her memories.

Staring at those cards, the memory of the last game she'd played with Adeline pulled Lydia into a daydream like quicksand stealing her away.

# CHAPTER THREE

The night Adeline died started like a dream and ended as a nightmare. The evening's card game between mother and child was a one-sided affair, with Adeline winning most hands. She beamed with happiness at her mother's defeat.

"I am terribly sorry for your *terrible* luck, Mama."

"You are clearly distraught over my poor play, little one."

They laughed together. Adeline exaggerated her cackle, drawing a sideways look from Wade on the porch. Lydia felt his quick glance through the closed screen door. He smiled at her over his paper. The front-page headline read, *Death Toll Reaches 15 in Texas Tower Shooting Rampage.* 1966 was shaping up to be a doozy of a year. She smiled back as she dropped her fan of losing cards.

"Okay, I'm done with you, kid. It's time to get in the tub. Let's go."

Adeline shot up and out of her chair with a burst of awkward grace that only young girls possess. She skipped across the room to the stairs, swung around on the banister, and disappeared upstairs in a blur of curls and song.

Lydia, much less graceful than her daughter, slowly stood, allowing her aging vertebrae to stack themselves one on the other at their own pace. She stretched her neck to the right, rubbing the left side with her open hand. She let a sigh escape her loose lips as she rotated on her heels toward the kitchen. She'd already had a long day, and she still had one last bout of cleaning to do before she joined Adeline upstairs for their goodnight ritual.

*Let's get this over with.*

As she stepped toward the sink basin, she heard the water filling the tub upstairs. Next, Adeline's feet scampered to her room, hopefully to gather her nightgown right on cue.

Lydia reflected on her day as she cleaned the counters. The summer's first thunderstorm had interrupted her time in the garden that afternoon. The sound of light rain tapping the porch roof floated through the screen door. The occasional flash of distant lightning caught her attention through the large window over the kitchen sink.

The clouds flashed over the trees behind the house. For a moment, the trees looked like dark giants against a glowing sky, rocking on their feet behind the home.

Lydia felt a sudden ominous swelling in her chest. Her hands, only moments ago busy cleaning, now lay still against the cool countertop. She had no reason to fear the weather; it was neither violent nor close.

Lydia heard Adeline enter the bathroom and shut the door. The young girl hummed to herself as the tub continued to fill. Adeline loved the water as close to full as possible. It drove Lydia and Wade nuts. Wade regularly complained about the waste of water and how Adeline only needed a fraction of it to wash her little body. Lydia didn't like Adeline filling the tub to its brim because that usually meant water on the floor and another mess to clean.

Lydia wasn't crazy about Adeline bathing in this weather, but she suspected her fear of lightning striking the house was a hangover from her youth. Someone convinced her mother that lightning could travel through the pipes and electrocute her mid-scrub. Lydia assumed it was possible. But probable? Not likely.

Lydia crossed the kitchen to the backdoor, nuzzling the screen door open with her shoulder as she toweled her wet hands.

"You should come in. It's getting late, and you can't see a thing out here."

A low laugh escaped the shadow in Wade's chair. "I'll be just another minute. I enjoy sitting out here and watching the lightning. You should join me."

"Adeline is in the tub. I don't want to be out of earshot while she's bathing."

She sensed Wade's smile in the dark. "Of course. You are the best mom. That girl wouldn't survive a week alone with me, especially with my poor decision-making skills."

She smiled and turned back into the house. Something caught her eye, and she froze.

*Is that water?*

On the stairs. Something moved. A shadow, or something else?

Her brain shifted into gear, convincing her feet to move. She walked briskly and felt nothing.

"Wade," she said in a slightly elevated but distracted voice.

*What is that?*

Lydia's breath caught in her chest as she reached the bottom of the staircase. Water slowly cascaded down the steps. It poured slowly but surely across, then down, then across, then down again. A puddle pooled around her feet.

She looked back up, panic taking hold of her as she attempted to understand what was happening.

Adeline, naked and wet, stood in the darkness at the top of the stairs. The bathroom door was closed behind her, a band of light fanning out from under the door. Adeline turned without saying a word and walked into her room.

"Adeline! What's happening? What are you doing?"

Lydia's instincts kicked in, and she flew up the wet stairs, calling more loudly for Wade as she went. She heard him coming through the screen door a world away, confusion in his voice.

"What's wrong? Lydia? Is that *water*? Dammit, the tub!"

Lydia ignored him, leaving the light behind as she entered the upstairs. Her eyes struggled to find edges and surfaces in the dark hall. She reached the landing and briskly entered Adeline's room. Inside, she stopped, tilting her head.

Lydia was alone.

Her mind filled with overwhelm as she struggled to comprehend what her eyes saw.

Adeline's room was just as she'd left it before dinner. Confused, Lydia turned and headed for the bathroom.

She blinked and arrived at the bathroom door. Water poured in a steady stream around her soaked socks. She felt her hand turn the warm doorknob as the world around her slowly unfolded.

Wade reached the top of the stairs, his words cut off suddenly. He stood frozen in the dark as Lydia opened the bathroom door.

The bright bathroom temporarily skewed her vision. Then she saw her.

Adeline floated face down in the tub, water pouring over the lip. Her chestnut brown hair spread out across the water around her head like the reaching pedals of a Velvet Queen Sunflower.

Lydia's legs felt cast in cement, her feet refusing to move as the world collapsed around her. She lost all sense of time.

She felt Wade pushing to get around her as her mouth hung open in a scream. The contact broke Lydia's paralysis. She and Wade both reached for Adeline, pulling her from the tub by her arms and waist.

Wade muttered, "No, no, no," repeatedly, the words melting into whimpers.

They went to the floor together, Wade cradling Adeline's limp, dripping body. Lydia ripped Adeline out of his arms, rolled her on her side, and pounded on her back with her open palm.

"Run! Get help!" she exclaimed.

Wade shot out of the bathroom and down the hall, apparently going for the phone in their bedroom.

This left Lydia alone, her daughter's unresponsive form beneath her hands. In a flurry of desperation, her fingers stumbled over Adeline's damp, youthful skin, as she fumbled to find a rhythm amidst her panic. She pressed her lips to Adeline's, forcing her own breath into the girl's silent mouth. Breath from mother to child. Water on everything. Pressing palms, tilted head, breathing, fuzzy vision, tingling fingers, compressions, breathing, shoulders tight, sobbing, loss, lost.

Lydia laid her head on Adeline's bare chest and sobbed helplessly. Seconds later, Lydia snapped up, lifting the girl into her arms. She squeezed her tight, trying to press her own life into Adeline. It was Lydia's last desperate attempt to pass life from her chest to the girl's. She would give it to her if God would allow it.

*Please, take me! Not her!*

She screamed as she squeezed her daughter with all her strength.

Lydia collapsed in desperation, exhausted and sobbing uncontrollably. The girl was gone, and she knew it.

Gone.

# CHAPTER FOUR

L ydia slowly returned from the memory. She sat at the kitchen table in her first moment of silent reflection since Adeline's death. Until today, the house had bustled with family and friends, comforting them through the traumatic ritual of burying their daughter. But today, with only her and Wade in the house, she finally found space to begin her grieving process.

How was she ever going to move past that night? Was it expected by the world that she would eventually move on, or is it assumed that parents of lost children will never recover? She couldn't imagine the former being possible.

Suddenly, the tears came flooding in a tsunami of emotion. Lydia put her head down and cried with her whole being. This moment had been a long time coming, and she needed it.

After several minutes, Lydia's mind drifted back to the present. Her sobbing ebbed from the surface, retreating steadily into the empty chasm within her. Lydia grabbed a napkin from the holder at the center of the table and wiped her tears away. Her exhales were deep and necessary. As she gathered her thoughts, the room around her came into focus, and her awareness returned.

Lydia realized she was truly in the greatest challenge of her life. Nothing compared to this.

Wade's footsteps crossed the ceiling above her as he made his way from their room to the stairs, the sound growing louder as he headed downstairs.

He reached the landing, stopped, and turned toward her, exhaling deeply with drooping shoulders. Lydia saw the remnants of his emotional release all over him. His eyes were red and swollen, revealing he'd also been crying.

"We're going to make it through this," Wade said, his voice wavering. He slowly approached the kitchen table. "Look, I'm sorry about earlier. I can't think clearly, and my mouth got the best of me. I'm sorry."

Lydia's eyes dropped from Wade to her hands, fingers twisting her napkin with anxious energy. Wade had taken a brave step by apologizing. Her appreciation for him as a gentle and caring man entered the spotlight in her mind.

"It's not your fault. We're both just—out of sorts. I didn't mean to spill your coffee. And I didn't mean to push you away last week. That must have felt awful. I'm sorry."

The silence stretched between them as each internally accepted the apology of the other.

"Hey, I thought it may be nice to take a cruise down 60 in the Valiant," Wade said, breaking the silence. "Getting some fresh air may do us some good."

Lydia held her response for a moment, her inner mourner outright refusing the offer. The manic voice pleaded with her.

*You don't want to do that. What if people see you out for a leisurely cruise? What will they think? You don't want people judging you right now, do you?*

The questions littered the front of Lydia's mind. However, her true hesitation festered at her core—she couldn't leave Adeline yet. Leaving the house felt like a giant leap toward moving on with life, and today was far too soon to consider any semblance of movement.

She shook her head to scatter the conflicting thoughts bounding around inside her, then surprised herself and probably Wade when she said, "Sure. That sounds nice."

As soon as the words left her mouth, she knew she'd lied to Wade. Why couldn't she just be honest with him? He was an understanding man. He wouldn't be upset if she declined the offer. Why couldn't she just say no?

*Because I need to try*, she thought.

"I'll go out and drop the top. I'll let you know when I'm ready, okay?"

"Sure."

She sensed Wade reading her face. She felt exposed. Could he tell she didn't really want to go? Would he press her further?

Before she could reconsider whether Wade believed her, he turned and walked through the backdoor to the porch. A moment later, she saw him methodically lowering the convertible top on the Plymouth.

She let out a trapped breath and looked around the room. How the heck was she going to get out of this without agitating Wade again? They had just put their morning confrontation behind them, and now she was jerking him around.

*You're a real mess, girl.*

Their 1965 Plymouth Valiant V-200 sat in the gravel driveway alongside the house, its top up to protect the white interior from the terrors of the Virginia summer. It was one of his favorite things in the world, a tidy little convertible with enough style to catch the eye without being overbearing. The very moment he saw the car on the lot at Al's Plymouth Chrysler Auto World on Route 60, he was hooked. He bought the car the next day on his way home from work and surprised his girls, rolling into the driveway beside the house with the top down and horn chirping in short, fun fits. Lydia had never seen him so smitten with a purchase before.

At first, Lydia had mixed emotions about the car. She loved the idea of wind-swept fall drives in a shiny new convertible, but where exactly was the money coming from to cover the monthly payment? They were barely making ends meet on his paper mill salary. Wade assured her he'd cornered Al into the greatest deal of the century, applying every trick he'd learned about buying cars from his old man. No one had been a better deal maker than Clyde "Stubby" Jones, and Wade had inherited his superior buying instincts. Lydia caved once she saw Adeline's excitement over the car. The girl absolutely loved it. That had been a year ago.

Lydia stood and walked to the back door. She reached for the doorknob and stopped, realizing her thirst for the first time in hours. She headed back to the kitchen sink and drew half a glass of water from the tap. Lydia closed her eyes and quickly gulped down the room-temperature well water. The residual taste of metal pipes lingered on her tongue as she opened her eyes and lowered the glass.

As she placed the glass in the sink, her eyes quickly scanned the yard beyond the kitchen window.

At the tree line, a set of eyes stared at Lydia.

She stopped in her tracks, her heartbeat pounding in her ears as her blood pressure climbed unchecked.

The eyes seemed to float among the green leaves of the ferns hugging the base of the trees where they met the yard.

Lydia could no longer sense the kitchen around her as her vision became fuzzy at its edges. She stared so intently, yet couldn't comprehend exactly what she was seeing. She refused to blink in fear of losing the eyes fixated on hers. Her left eye watered.

Wade's voice dashed her trance to pieces. "Ready to go when you are." He had somehow crossed the porch and entered the back door without Lydia noticing him.

Lydia startled as her eyes shot to the back door. Realizing that Wade had come for her, she panicked for just a split second. She scrambled to find the eyes lingering on the tree line through the kitchen window again.

Nothing. There was nothing there. No eyes, no child, no animal. The trees stood their watch over the yard like disciplined sentries.

"Are you okay?" Wade asked with genuine concern.

"Yeah, I—I'm sorry." Images of the eyes scattered in all directions in Lydia's mind. Her eyes surveyed the yard again, taking their last opportunity to convince her mind that nothing was out of the ordinary beyond the home.

"You don't look so hot." Wade went to her, placing his hand on her left elbow as if to steady her.

"No, I'm fine. I promise. I just thought I saw an animal in the yard, and I got a little worked up. You know how the deer like to eat my hostas. They wiped them out last year before we ever saw their purple blooms." She looked him in the eye.

"I'm good."

She wasn't sure Wade bought her story, but he didn't press her. "Okay. Are you still good with going for a drive?"

"Actually, I'm not sure I'm up for it. I think my lack of sleep is getting to me. Would you be upset if I stayed back and took a nap? Please don't let that stop *you* from going."

Lydia noticed the struggle behind Wade's eyes. Although he did a good job of hiding his disappointment, he looked conflicted. She knew he really needed to get out and clear his head, but he would never leave her if she was upset.

She spoke up, more confidently this time. "You should go. Really. I'll be okay here."

"That's fine," he said, looking both conflicted and re-lieved.

Lydia turned and placed her hands on his chest. It was the closest they'd been to each other without crying in over a week.

"Be safe and enjoy some time alone. I'll be here when you get back." She leaned in and pressed her forehead to his lips.

Lydia closed her eyes and stayed with him for just another moment before stepping back and allowing his passage to the backdoor. As Wade walked across the back porch to the driveway, Lydia stole a quick glance through the window toward the tree line. As the Valiant roared to life in the driveway, she accepted that the eyes she'd seen had been a product of a tired and stressed mind.

Maybe so, but the image of them burned in the back of her mind all the same.

# CHAPTER FIVE

Lydia watched from the front window as Wade eased the Valiant out of the gravel drive, its engine's hum soothing her through the walls of the house. Within seconds, the car sped out of view.

She was alone. *Very* alone. She felt vulnerable. An anxious tension blossomed behind her breastbone.

Lydia turned to the home's interior, the sheer drapes swaying into place where she stood just a moment before. She walked to the stairs and paused before commencing her ascent. She looked up the wooden steps. Beyond them, the doors to the bathroom and Adeline's bedroom flanked the landing like watchmen. Lydia's heart sank as she considered passing between them to the primary bedroom down the hall. She lowered her eyes, exhaled wearily as she gathered her confidence, and took the steps one at a time.

As she reached the landing, she tried to stay focused on her destination, but her eyes refused to obey. The hall was dark, but light emitted from Adeline's room. Beyond the bedroom's threshold, Lydia saw a tidy and youthful room of pastels and plush surfaces. They were the trappings of a girl who would never grace the room again. The light pink comforter of the bed reflected the sun's rays onto the light walls, filling the space with life. Stuffed animals arranged on Adeline's shelves stared back, delightful and welcoming. The closet door remained closed, the dresser top's items organized, everything in its right place. Lydia breathed deeply, pulled her eyes away, and ventured into the hall's shadows. She couldn't remember ever being this drawn to her bed. Her pending nap was nonnegotiable.

Lydia entered her room, avoiding the light switch as she kicked off her house shoes and climbed into their bed. Cool linen sheets greeted her with a chilling embrace. Lydia rolled onto her side, facing toward the bedroom door and away from the curtained windows. No light entered the room except for a few stray rays which found their way around the edges and seams of the curtains behind her. She closed her eyes, welcoming the darkness.

A voice crept into her mind, wedging itself between the land of the sleeping and the sleepless.

*Will you visit her soon? It's been over twenty-four hours since your last visit. She's been alone this whole time.*

The voice in her head aroused the memory machine. Images of Adeline's grave materialized behind Lydia's shut eyes. The granite headstone rose defiantly from the dirt at the child's head. The sun speckled the face of the tombstone between the shadows of leaves from surrounding trees. She felt like she was standing mere feet away from the mound of fresh soil blanketing Adeline's resting place. The vision was relentless and cruel, pushing ice water into every pore of her body.

She felt further from sleep than she was when she entered the room. She *had to* still her mind and push the visions away, or sleep would evade her.

Right on cue, her mind flashed to several days before when she lay in the same bed, trying to achieve the same impossible feat. That was the day the gravediggers came.

*Oh God, no. Please don't do this,* she thought.

It was no use begging. The memory of that day flashed forward, dashing the tombstone from her mind's eye.

The day before the funeral, Lydia laid in her bed, trying miserably to nap. Her head ached with exhaustion from several days of poor sleep and a lacking appetite.

She heard a truck pull into the driveway. The muffled sound of Wade's voice met those of several men from town. The men spoke in low, brief exchanges, trying their best to avoid unnecessary conversation.

The muffled voices migrated to the backyard as the workers moved their tools to the copse of trees behind the home. The family graveyard played a distinguished role in their lives, hidden down a path behind the yard. Several generations of Lydia's family lay there, now residents of the unknown beyond the known. Digging the grave with shovels was the only option because of the tight path in the dense trees. There was no way to get a machine back there to make light work of the dark undertaking.

Lydia laid in the dark room, practically begging God to grant her sleep, but their work became a soundtrack for her daydreams. The sounds of shovels striking the earth, cutting clay, and tossing soil aside poured into her mind until she thought she'd go mad. Her head throbbed with the intensity of the sound. She felt as if she lay at the diggers' feet, her body pressed to the soil battered by their spades. When their work was done, they could plant a foot on her back and shove her into the grave, sparing Adeline from burial. Then, the shovels could return to their rhythmic tasks and seal her within the earth forever.

She never found rest that afternoon.

Hours later, after sunset, Wade found Lydia standing in the dark kitchen, staring out across the backyard. He went to her and, without a word, wrapped his arms around her and cried. The day had been hard on him, too. He did his best, trying to be a loving husband, but he had nothing left to give.

His cry was the kind a man rarely let the world see. For the entirety of her life, hearing a man cry like that moved Lydia to immediate concern. She'd only seen her father cry that deeply twice in her youth, once when his mother passed and again when his father followed her into death many years later.

On that night, in that world without her daughter, Lydia realized she and Adeline had each received an eternal gift. The mother bore a wound that would never heal, and the daughter received God's acre.

As Wade's tears spread on the shoulder of her nightgown, Lydia stood with her arms hanging at her sides, saying nothing. She stared over his shoulder, through the window, at the trees guarding the cemetery. Behind those trees was a grave dug especially for her child.

That black hole in the ground spoke to her under a sky intermittently illuminated by summer's heat lightning. *She'll be mine soon.*

Lydia's anger simmered at her core. Her little girl was one night closer to being gone forever.

The next day, they buried the child. That godforsaken black hole finally got what it wanted, permanently entombing Adeline within the earth. She was forever out of sight and reach, and Lydia's mind couldn't comprehend that reality.

She would never resign Adeline to the earth forever. Somehow, she would see her again.

She believed that with every fiber of her being.

Lydia opened her eyes to the bedroom's darkness. She couldn't sleep. She had to get out of that room.

Sitting up, she swung her legs from under the sheets, and searched the dark floor with her feet for her slippers. Her feet found them, and she stood and walked from the room to the hall with no idea what to do next.

No sleep. No rest. Just frustration to cloud her thoughts.

Lydia stopped at the partially open door to Adeline's room. She eased the door open the rest of the way. The door's hinges protested mildly, notifying the room's inhabitants of her pending entrance.

Her eyes panned the room, stumbling over the memories living in each trinket, childhood drawing taped to the wall, and stuffed animal. So much of Adeline was there, suspended in inanimate objects beloved by the girl over years of youthful play. Lydia felt her guard drop a bit as she calmed her nerves and reflected on the beautiful life Adeline had built in her nine years of life. Simple joys, innocent affection, the creative expressions of a young girl yet to experience the cruelties of life.

It really was beautiful.

Lydia sat on the edge of Adeline's bed.

She saw Adeline's favorite childhood book, *Goodnight Moon*, on the nightstand beside her. Adeline loved that book and frequently read it before bed, always with a smile.

"I can't believe you still read that book," Lydia would say. And Adeline always replied with, "You are never too old to say goodnight to the moon."

Smiling, Lydia felt the pull of sleep once again. The room had eased her nerves. Being among Adeline's possessions relieved her tension.

Lydia hesitated for a moment, then laid her head on Adeline's pillow. She smelled traces of the girl everywhere around her. As she closed her eyes, Adeline's glowing face greeted her. She was all smiles and curls. Her voice carried to Lydia's mind over a chasm of time and space.

*Rest your heart, Mama. I'm here in your dreams.*

This was the closest Lydia had been to Adeline since her passing. The soothing familiarity loosened the chords pulling Lydia's insides taught. Her stress dissipated with each passing moment immersed in Adeline's memory.

Lydia's breathing deepened. Her relaxing body sunk further into the mattress.

Finally, sleep consumed her.

# CHAPTER SIX

Lydia eased her eyes open to the sound of footsteps in the hall. For a moment, she was unsure whether she was waking from a dream or still trapped inside one. Her mind rifled through its files, segregating dream visions from memories of the day's events. She blinked her eyes, doing her best to clear the fog of sleep.

She was warm and settled in the comfort of Adeline's bed. The sunlight pressed through the drapes covering the window, casting pastel colors and indistinct shapes across every surface of the room.

The door was slightly ajar, holding the line between the brightened room and the shadows of the home. Lydia heard a door close softly somewhere in the hall. The padded reverberations of bare feet transiting the wood floors departed earshot.

She wasn't sure how long she'd napped, but apparently, it was long enough for Wade to complete his trip down Route 60 and back. She hoped his drive was as restorative to Wade as her nap was to her.

*He's probably looking for me. Will he be upset that I slept in here?*

Lydia rolled onto her back, blinked her eyes a few times, and considered what she'd say when she encountered Wade in the hall.

That's when the Valiant came rumbling into the driveway.

Outside, the convertible idled beside the house for a few seconds before the engine quieted abruptly. The dampened sound of a car door closing drove another note of confirmation into her mind. That was *definitely* Wade in the driveway.

"Hello?" she asked the silence of the upstairs.

No answer.

Wade walked through the backdoor of the home. He called out to Lydia, "I'm home." She heard his keys land in the basket on the kitchen counter.

The upstairs was silent.

*It was just your imagination. You were waking from a dream, that's all.*

Lydia felt the sudden urge to leave the room before Wade made his way upstairs. She wasn't sure how he'd feel about her napping in Adeline's bed. After the morning they'd had, she didn't want to cause another conflict.

"On my way down," she said, her voice elevated and shaky. She stood, straightened the pillow and comforter, and took a moment's glance around the room before opening the door. She felt like she was getting away with something, although she had nothing to hide.

As she reached the bottom of the stairs, she found Wade sitting at the kitchen table. He pried his shoes off, one foot at a time, and acknowledged her with a half-smile. She saw some relief on his face at the sight of her. She gave a small smile back.

His smile said, *I had a good drive, and I'm happy you are here.* Her smile said, *I had a good nap. I'm glad you are back.* Neither of them said a word.

Lydia walked into the kitchen, feeling a little lighter than she had in days. The house felt better, *cooler*, than it had that morning. She'd really needed that nap.

"Coffee?" she asked.

"That sounds great," Wade said approvingly.

"It looks like you had a good drive. How did the car run?" Lydia asked, making small talk.

"Oh, it needed that drive after sitting for the past week and a half. It pepped right up once I got on 60."

"Good." She finished the coffee pot preps.

"Were you able to rest while I was gone?" Wade asked.

"Yes. I needed that nap more than I knew. I had a hard time falling asleep at first," she stopped herself, choosing her story's ending carefully. "But I eventually fell asleep."

"That's good." He wrinkled his brow, slightly worried looking. Then the worry was gone, almost as if he became aware he was showing his hand. "Well, I'm positive we'll have our good and bad days, but hopefully, we can somehow learn how to make a little progress each day."

Lydia turned away, shielding her face for a moment. An unexpected anger bloomed in her.

*What the hell is he thinking? Progress? Good days?*

Lydia couldn't fathom such things. On one hand, she knew things would get progressively easier, but on the other, much heavier hand, there was no room for that talk this soon.

"I left something upstairs," she said, feeling tension build in her shoulders and neck. "I'll be right back."

She gave Wade no chance to ask questions. Lydia walked with a purpose up the stairs, being careful not to stomp her feet and blow her cover. She wasn't sure if Wade realized his poor choice of words. Now, she really didn't care what he realized. She needed a few minutes to calm herself, and the small bathroom attached to their bedroom seemed like the perfect place for it.

As Lydia approached the top of the stairs, she noticed something from the corner of her eye.

The door to Adeline's bedroom.

*The door was open when I left the room. I didn't close it, did I?*

Apparently, she had. Before she thought any further, Lydia turned the doorknob and pushed the door open.

She looked inquisitively about the room. Everything was in its right place.

*Everything but my sweet girl*, she thought bitterly.

Lydia turned to continue her walk to the primary bedroom when she felt an unexpected calm wash over her.

She couldn't breathe. She stood there, eyes closed, suspended in the moment, relief coursing through her body.

*Why had she been so worked up? Where was she going?* She couldn't remember.

Slowly turning toward the stairs, Lydia abandoned her original destination in favor of returning to the kitchen.

*What was I coming upstairs for, anyway?*

Whatever it was, it wasn't important. She was on her way back to the kitchen. Back to Wade. Back to the fresh coffee brewing in the pot.

As Lydia entered the kitchen, she did her best to hide her weightlessness. She felt as if she were gliding.

She felt Wade watching her closely.

"So, what was it?" he asked.

"What was what?" she replied.

"What was it you forgot upstairs?" he finished, a note of curiosity hanging on his last word.

Lydia paused, collecting her thoughts, her brow slightly furrowed. She couldn't recall *what* she had gone upstairs for. She'd gone and come back, but what for?

*Make something up*, she thought urgently. Her sense of numb weightlessness dissipated quickly. She was crashing back into the reality of the kitchen.

"Um, I left the light on in our bathroom earlier. I needed to turn it off."

*There's no way he's buying that.* However, she couldn't think of anything better to say. She sure as hell wasn't going to tell him she left before her temper got the best of her and that she'd had a strange and unexplained experience in Adeline's room.

"Of course." Wade flashed a shallow smile again.

Changing the topic, Lydia said, "I think I'll spend a little time weeding the vegetable garden before starting supper."

Wade nodded. "Sounds good. I'll put the top up on the car and work in the shed while you're in the yard."

---

They spent the remaining afternoon in the sun. Lydia enjoyed every minute of her time in her garden. She tended to her tomatoes, string beans, and cucumbers. Gardening lifted Lydia's spirits and brought her a unique sense of accomplishment and connectedness with the earth. Her yard was her sanctuary, especially now with Adeline gone.

Now, as Lydia pulled weeds and turned soil, she stole occasional glances across the yard to the path in the woods. Each time, her heart momentarily stumbled, her mind pulling her down the short path to Adeline.

*I can't do that. I need to stay in the moment.*

The day had been strange enough already. She needed to keep herself grounded.

After a few hours, Lydia made her way into the house to clean up and prepare supper. Wade appeared a few minutes before the meal was ready.

They filled their plates with baked chicken, spinach, and buttered rolls before resting in adjacent chairs at the table. They ate quietly, their silence inspired by deep hunger.

Spending the afternoon outdoors had done wonders for their appetites.

After dinner, Lydia washed the dishes while Wade retired to the porch for his evening cigar. She suspected he read the paper that evening, more so as a matter of habit than interest, perhaps trying to keep his routine and his sanity in the process.

After drying and shelving the evening's dishes and cookware, Lydia wiped down the counters and dried the surface around the sink. Finishing her last pass, she took a moment to stand at the sink and watch the path winding into the woods.

The trees swayed rhythmically in the dusk breeze. In mere moments, she became entranced by the kaleidoscopic effect of the moving leaves and shifting greens. She felt her vision being pulled deep into the whirlpool of vegetation. Reveling in the moment, Lydia felt at peace. She also experienced something almost calming as the world blended with a realm beyond the real. Lydia felt like she was in two places at once.

She realized nothing would ever be the same again. How? She wasn't sure. However, she knew the world had moved on, taking her somewhere beyond her comprehension, and there was nothing she could do to stop it.

# CHAPTER SEVEN

The night crashed on both Lydia and Wade earlier and harder than usual, a tsunami of mental and emotional exhaustion propelled by the gravity of the day.

After cleaning the kitchen, Lydia retreated to the bedroom for the night. She felt completely drained.

As she climbed into bed, Wade entered the room, passed her quietly, and closed the bathroom door behind him. He would emerge in a few minutes to join her, but she wasn't sure she'd still be awake by the time he was done.

She closed her eyes to pull a shade over the wide band of light glowing from under the bathroom door. Lydia exhaled deeply, welcoming sleep. Her thoughts drifted to her garden in the backyard. In her mind, she pictured flowers dancing in the twilight. The rhythm of their sway transfixed her mind's eye. Exhaustion pulled her further into the darkness like weights around her ankles.

She slipped into the depths of sleep, the image of those flowers dancing in her mind.

Lydia opened her eyes to the sound of a door closing in the hall. She saw the bedroom surrounding her as a world of blacks and grays in the moonlight drifting through the partially shaded window.

*What time is it? Is Wade in bed?*

She felt the warmth of his body inches from hers under the sheets. She heard his deep breathing and registered him as *very* asleep. Wade always slept hard. Lydia often joked that he could sleep through the Apocalypse.

Clearly, she had slept for some time before waking. But for how long?

She heard nothing in the hall. Perhaps she'd awoken by a dream that she couldn't recall in the moment.

She lay there, easing her heart rate and seeking clues in the night with her eyes and ears.

Nothing.

Closing her eyes again, she welcomed a return to the depths of sleep, the heavy blanket of the day still weighing her down.

Lydia's eyes shot open. She heard a familiar sound through the closed bedroom door.

Water running into the hall tub.

She sat up quietly, convinced she was awash in the receding waves of a dream.

The sound persisted. She eased her legs out from under the covers and placed her feet on the throw rug beside the bed.

She paused, listening intently. *I'm not crazy. There is water running in the tub*, she thought.

Lydia stood slowly, careful to reduce the impact of her rising from the mattress. Under normal circumstances, she'd quickly wake Wade and make him aware of significant sounds in the house at night. However, this time, she avoided his involvement. She was more curious than scared.

After all, she was not convinced this wasn't a dream. Bad guys don't break into houses to take baths. This was something different.

Her heartbeat increased with every quietly placed step across the room. She stood at the bedroom door, hand on the knob, and leaned forward to press her ear to the door.

She heard more than running water through the wooden door. She heard *life*.

Lydia's heart rate climbed. Adrenaline coursed through her veins, elevating her senses and sharpening her mind.

With little thought, she quietly turned the doorknob in her hand.

Lydia entered another reality in the hallway.

At the other end of the dark corridor, light emanated from beneath two closed doors—Adeline's bedroom and the hall bathroom.

The bedroom emitted warm pink light and a muffled hum. In the bathroom, cool white light and the therapeutic tumble of running water. Warm, moist air blanketed her exposed skin and settled into her nightclothes.

She froze to contemplate what she observed. Her mind pinballed between memories from the day. The magical feel of laying on Adeline's bed. The overwhelming sense of calm at the girl's bedroom door.

The eyes watching from the trees.

*Okay, breathe. You aren't in danger—I don't think.*

These things shouldn't be happening. *Nothing* should happen at God-knows-what-time-in-the-morning.

Logic gained ahold of Lydia's mind, and she opened her mouth to call Wade's name when she froze.

The door to Adeline's room opened.

If someone threatening had invaded their home, it was now too late to go undetected. She loomed large in the hall, frozen in place but clearly visible to anyone entering the space. Confrontation was imminent.

Fight or flight. Rush or dash. The time was now.

In the manic seconds since the door opened, Lydia's mind had stalled every muscle of her body. Her eyes were the only moving thing on her. And what they saw next, well, she couldn't comprehend.

Wet footprints appeared on the hardwood floor, one ahead of the other, stepping from Adeline's bedroom to the bathroom door. A moist slapping sound presented each footprint on the polished planks.

The bathroom door opened, stopped for a few seconds, then shut without incident.

Lydia nearly fell dead right where she stood. Her heart pounded so hard that the percussions drowned out all other sounds. Tears raced down each cheek.

*It's her.*

Lydia's body filled with heat as her emotions burst forth. Fear mixed with love, and disbelief mixed with overwhelm.

Her mind detached from her body. Her numb legs slowly took one step forward, then another, then stopped.

She choked back a deluge of tears, stifling her breathing with a cupped hand. She feared interrupting her daughter.

*If* that's who was in the bathroom.

Her detached body took another step forward, then stopped as movement in the bathroom began.

She strained to comprehend the sound.

Thrashing.

In the tub.

*Adeline* thrashing in the tub.

A scream blasted up from Lydia's feet to her mouth, threatening to erupt from her in an uncontrollable, horrific shrill.

Her hand flew to her mouth, and she pressed her tongue to the roof like a vise.

*You choke on that scream, or she'll leave you forever.*

The hall spiraled before her as the thrashing in the tub suddenly subsided.

*What's done is done. It's too late to save her now*, she thought.

Lydia's vision steadied, her sobs eased, and she wrestled her mind into submission.

*Breathe. Breathe.*

She knew what she had to do. She had to check the bathroom.

As Lydia planned her next steps in her mind, she heard the water draining. Someone—Adeline—must have pulled the plug.

As the tub emptied, Lydia stood paralyzed. She strained to hear whatever happened ahead of her.

The bathroom went dark, its light flickering off. Adeline's bedroom went dark. The wet footprints appeared in the hall again. This time, they stepped from the bathroom door to the stairs.

Down the steps, they went.

Lydia moved.

She arrived at the top of the landing as the footprints reached the downstairs floor and turned toward the back of the house.

This time, Lydia moved with more awareness, careful not to disturb the wet footprints soaking each stair.

She met the main floor and raced beside the footprints to the backdoor where they vanished.

She never saw the door open, never heard another sound.

*The window. Go to the window,* the voice in her mind demanded.

She stepped over the wet footprints and rushed to the kitchen window. In the dark, she leaned over the sink, straining her eyes to scan the porch.

That's when she saw Adeline for the first time.

A dense white shadow of Adeline's form walked slowly from the porch to the path in the woods. With each step, her form dimmed a notch.

A whimper escaped Lydia as she stood frozen at the sink, every inch of her face a quivering billboard of emotion. Love poured from her shaking breast.

*I can't believe it. I* must *believe it.*

Just before Adeline's ghost reached the trees, she appeared to look back at Lydia.

*She sees me. My God, she sees me.*

A breeze swept the yard, stimulating every branch, flower, and soul.

Then, Adeline was gone.

# CHAPTER EIGHT

L ydia stood under the moonlight in the backyard. Her face felt frozen, her mouth slightly agape. Her thoughts skipped like a fouled needle on a record as she struggled to grasp what she'd seen.

*Who* she'd seen.

She felt exposed and exhilarated. Seeing Adeline's ghost just moments before left her in shock.

*It was her. My God, it was her.*

Adrenaline pressed her senses to their limits. She looked and listened, hoping to catch a glimpse or hear a word. She stood still and attentive, the moon full, bright, and alone in the night sky above her.

*Should I go to her? Should I walk the path to the gravesite? What if she's there, waiting for me?*

The logic police in Lydia's mind raised from their slumber and cast doubt over what her eyes had reported from the kitchen. The list of arguments against observing the ghost of a dead girl stacked quickly and neatly in her head.

*Don't be absurd. You were dreaming. You are exhausted and still in shock. You'd better get back to bed before Wade wakes. Good luck explaining* any *of this to him.*

The less critical creatures of her mind spoke up in mild protest.

*You know what you heard, what you saw. It was so real, all of it—the thrashing in the tub, the wet footprints, Adeline's ghost in the yard. You've never dreamed so vividly in your life. You may want it to be a dream, so you don't think you're going crazy. You're trying to protect your sanity. You saw what you saw.*

The logical voice put their foot down.

*We're not doing this. Which do you think is more probable: Adeline reliving her death, or you dreaming it up? It was a dream. It had to be.*

That settled it. Lydia exhaled past shaky lips, a hint of conflicted hope cradling her heart. Her head hurt, and her body felt weak as the adrenaline wore off. Healing from the loss of Adeline suddenly felt more impossible than it had at any moment since the girl's death.

Lydia walked back to the house, glancing over her shoulder once to convince herself there was nothing and no one to see out there under the summer moon.

As she made her way across the porch and into the house, she became more and more convinced that she'd dreamed the entire experience. Her mind cleared a little more with each step.

She locked the back door behind her and walked upstairs, her exhaustion pulling her toward slumber.

She suddenly remembered the wet footprints she'd avoided on her way to the kitchen earlier. Her eyes shot to the floor, a brief surge of anticipation landing squarely in her chest.

Nothing. If there were wet footprints before, they were no longer visible.

*Where are they? Did I really imagine them? How was that so vivid, so real?*

She became further convinced the night had been a cruel dream. She'd been so overwhelmed with wonder, fear, excitement, and love. Now, cold disappointment and brutal reality set in. Adeline was gone for good. She may be a spirit somewhere, but it wasn't here. The spirits of departed children belong somewhere far better than this hell of an existence. This is a place for the remnants, the bitter and grief-stricken parents of the departed.

*It should have been me who died. Why wasn't I the one who had the seizure in the tub? Why did it have to be her?*

As she walked up the stairs, Lydia's thoughts burrowed deeper into the ugly mire of depression. With each step, she piled on, plunging her outlook further under the soil of despair, further from light, further from sustainable life.

Lydia lifted her eyes as she neared the top steps. The dark hall ahead came into sight. On the right, warm light spilled from Adeline's bedroom.

Lydia stopped on the third step from the top, struggling to understand what she saw. The voice that spent the last ten minutes convincing her the night had been a dream lost all credibility as Lydia's eyes took in the evidence before her.

Adeline's bedroom was alive with an ethereal glow. Lydia floated into the chamber of light.

She stood in Adeline's room, basking in the same surreal emotion she'd experienced earlier that afternoon. Her eyes panned around the room. Everything remained in its proper place. However, she sensed *something* in the room. The air felt altered, substantial. Every breath tasted sweet. Lydia heard a barely audible tone in the air. She couldn't put her finger on it. She heard it with her mind, not her ears.

*I can't believe this. I feel like I'm somewhere else entirely.*

She realized she couldn't identify the light source. The lamps were off, and the moon, although bright in the sky, hovered above the opposite side of the home. Its light did little to breach the curtains.

After what she'd experienced in the hall earlier, this encounter felt mild and acceptable. She almost didn't care where the light came from.

Lydia closed her eyes. The light pulsed faintly, and she smiled. "Is that you, baby?"

*Come, lay down. Rest*, said a voice in and around her.

Lydia eased her weary body onto the bed. She felt the cool pillow wrap around her head as she allowed her weight to settle. She closed her eyes as Adeline's voice enveloped her thoughts.

*Believe. You didn't dream a thing. I saw you and you saw me. And it was beautiful. I miss you, Mama.*

"I miss you too, baby," Lydia breathed the words into the room.

The smell of Adeline's freshly washed hair and precious young skin blessed Lydia's senses.

"I love you more than life itself, Adeline. I'll see you in our dreams, little one. Adventures await us on the other side. You and me, we'll dance on the moon and kiss the clouds. The dark doesn't stand a chance against us."

As Lydia slipped into slumber, Adeline leaned into her ear and whispered, "I'll be there waiting for you."

Lydia felt someone standing over her. She opened her eyes to see Wade, and a room kissed by sunlight.

"Hey," he said softly as he cleared the concern from his face.

Lydia tried to prop herself up on her elbows. "Oh, hey. I'm sorry, I couldn't sleep, and I ended up in here. I guess I fell asleep."

*Don't you dare mention a word about last night,* she thought. She wasn't prepared to make sense of what she'd seen and heard, let alone explain it to Wade.

Lydia awaited Wade's reaction while she rubbed her eyes and sat up fully. She wanted to swing her legs out of bed, but Wade inadvertently blocked her passage to the left. He leaned in, his eyebrows drawn tight despite his attempt to hide his reaction to finding her sleeping in Adeline's bed.

Wade looked down at a small picture frame on Adeline's nightstand. The frame held a pencil drawing of a teddy bear wearing a scarf. Adeline had drawn the picture several years ago in the second grade. She'd been obsessed with creating art from the day she'd first held a crayon.

He looked deflated as he stared at the drawing, his stature diminished and weak. She saw a flash of deep despair in his reddening eyes. He quickly cleared the emotion from his face. She wondered if he was genuinely interested in reflecting on the drawing or simply upset and avoiding eye contact.

His eyes returned to Lydia's. He seemed to force a half-smile and spoke in softer tones.

"It's okay. Uh, I'm going to make coffee and get the day started. You should join me. We slept a little longer than usual."

He turned and walked out of the room before Lydia could respond.

# CHAPTER NINE

As the late morning sun warmed the surrounding air, Lydia and Wade sipped their coffee in silence on the screened back porch. She couldn't believe they'd slept so deeply into the day. They'd finally paid their penance for the turbulence of the previous days and nights.

Drawing energy and heat from the coffee in her hands, Lydia broke the silence. "How did you sleep?"

"Like a stone. It was like I time jumped from the moment I laid down to the time I opened my eyes this morning."

*That's insane*, Lydia thought. *How is it possible that I've been experiencing all this without you? The sensations in Adeline's room, the wild thrashing in the hall bath, the pas-*

*sage of Adeline's spirit through the home. All of it. Just for me?*

Suddenly concerned that Wade could see the secrets through her facial expression, she quickly looked up to find him none the wiser. He gazed across the backyard, looking as docile and unassuming as ever.

*Tell him what's been going on.*

Lydia almost scoffed aloud at the thought but caught herself. How exactly would that conversation go? *Hey! I know this is an odd question, but have you really not heard me chasing your daughter's ghost around the house for the past two days?*

She cleared her throat and sat up. Wade turned toward her, perhaps thinking she was trying to get his attention.

*Don't you dare say a word to him*, she thought a mere second before opening her mouth.

"Have you noticed anything, I don't know, different about the house the past day or so?" As soon as the words left her mouth, she felt embarrassed.

"I don't think so. What do you mean?"

Lydia dropped her eyes to her coffee cup, wishing it were a mile deeper so she could climb into it and hide.

"I don't know. I'm actually not sure what I'm trying to say." She exhaled, sifting frantically through her mind for the words to tell him what she'd experienced. "It sounds crazy, but every time I go into Adeline's room, I feel like I'm—somewhere else. It's like a soothing calm comes over me. Have you felt that?" She bit her tongue to prevent furthering the damage.

Wade turned his focus back to the yard and sighed. "I wanted to talk with you about this but wasn't sure how to bring it up."

*He's choosing his words very carefully and avoiding eye contact*, she thought. *Is he holding back tears?*

Wade clenched his jaw. "I didn't want to say anything because I didn't want to upset you. I know you napped in her room yesterday. I noticed the bedding was disturbed after I returned from my drive. But you never mentioned that you'd napped there instead of our room. When I woke up alone this morning, I knew I'd find you in there again."

"I want you to be honest with me," Wade continued, "and God knows I'm right here with you, dying inside without Adeline. I'm bitter and angry. I don't know why this had to happen. I don't know why He took her from us."

Lydia looked up to see him fighting back tears. His lower lip quivered as he wiped his eyes.

"All I know is that I can't lose you, too. And I'm afraid that losing Adeline may kill us both."

He looked directly at her. She met his eyes and without hesitation said, "I've seen her."

The tension between them became static in her ears. Heat replaced her guilt. She let her thoughts flow into words.

"I know it sounds crazy, but I *saw* her. She's still here." She pressed him with her eyes, trying to convince him.

Wade looked down at his hands, leaving Lydia unsure how he would respond to her proclamation.

He leaned into his words carefully. "We'll get through this one day at a time. What else can we do? But I need you to tell me if you aren't alright. You *have* to promise me. If you need help, please tell me."

Lydia furrowed her brow. "What are you saying? Do you think I'm going crazy?"

Wade raised his hands in defense. "I didn't say that. I—"

"Yeah, but you implied it. I don't need help. I need *time*. I need her."

She stood and walked into the house.

———

Lydia spent the next hour avoiding contact with Wade. She moved briskly from room to room, adjusting this thing, dusting that thing. She stayed busy doing nothing. Where their paths crossed, Wade honored her by steering clear of conversation.

Seeking fresh air and separation, Lydia emerged from the house to tend to her garden. She needed to go to her thinking place outside under the sun, with the breeze, and closer to nature.

While she gardened, she tossed the conversation with Wade around the walls of her mind. She felt conflicted. She was grateful that Wade cared about her. He was a good, loving husband. She couldn't fault him for being concerned, especially after she'd admitted to seeing Adeline. But his inability to simply listen and trust her mild account frustrated her.

*I should have kept my mouth shut*, she thought. *We could have had a decent day, but now the odds of that happening appear slim. Why didn't I keep that to myself?*

She knew the answer—she was excited about Adeline's return. Somehow, she wanted him to experience that with her. However, she seriously misjudged Wade's readiness to have that conversation. He was a loving, supportive husband, but he was also in mourning and very concerned for his wife.

*Why did he immediately dismiss me? He didn't even try to believe.*

Perhaps she also misjudged whether Wade *should* have that conversation. After all, Adeline avoided him, making her presence known only to Lydia. Maybe Adeline knew Wade wasn't ready to believe, so she'd protected him.

Lydia set her tools down and stared into the churned bed before her. She closed her eyes, tilted her head to the sky, and eased her hands into the moist soil, adoring the cool, damp sponginess. She let out a shaky breath and opened her mind's eye to whatever may come. Sunlight fought to breach her closed eyelids, but only imprinted orange patterns in her shielded vision.

Then, the whispering arrived.

*I'm all yours. I'll always be yours. We are inseparable. The night presents our union. Time and earth will press us together, one body, forever.*

*I see you. I need you. Together, tonight. Be there for me.*

Lydia's pulse created rhythmic percussions in her wrists, neck, head, and feet. She hypnotically swayed, fully immersed in blissful warmth. Her chest ached with love and longing.

Lydia spoke to her. "Oh, Adeline. Come back to me, sweet girl. I need to see you again."

*Shhh.*

Deep in the chambers of her mind, a voyage unfolded. In this vision, she walked down the path to Adeline's grave, running her hands through the wild ferns along the path. The sky grew darker with each step. As she reached the family cemetery, there was barely enough light in the sky to make out the trees. There, standing prominently above Adeline's freshly buried plot, was a large white clawfoot tub. The headstones of her departed parents and several aunts, uncles, and cousins guarded the clearing. The persistence of time had assembled the family here.

A hum filled her ears, pulling her toward the tub. The sound coursed through her like electricity, a direct and unrelenting native frequency broadcast from somewhere beyond the living. Lydia, now naked, slowly lifted one foot, remnants of the path clinging to her moist skin. As her begrimed toes met the hot water's surface, a whisper so present and so real ripped her back to the garden.

"Soon. Open your eyes, Mama."

Lydia's eyes shot open to see clouds swallowing the sun whole. It was beautiful. She looked around and found the yard in its usual state. She inhaled a lungful of the humid floral atmosphere and looked toward the path to the cemetery. A seed of anxious energy held a small flame of excitement within her core.

Adeline was trying to tell her something. Lydia would follow the day where it took her as long as it led to another night with Adeline.

She stood with conviction in her eyes and made her way back to the house.

# CHAPTER TEN

Lydia entered the house through the back door and found Wade waiting for her at the kitchen table. Stacked on the table in a tidy column before him were his checkbook, a few bills, and his notebook from the mill. A black ballpoint pen tumbled nimbly between the fingers of his right hand as he read a letter held in his left. He set the letter and the pen down at the sight of Lydia.

"Hey, I hope you don't mind, but I need to go into town for a bit. I need to bring the Valiant by Al's for an annual inspection. After that, I need to stop by the mill to discuss my schedule with Jim. Is that okay with you?"

"Of course," she replied with a forced uplift in her voice. "Don't feel pressured to rush home. I've got laundry and cleaning to do. I'd stay outside in the yard a bit longer, but it's getting pretty hot out there." She faked a smile, pulled a short glass from the kitchen cabinet, and walked to the refrigerator to pour a cold glass of iced tea.

"Yeah, I'd better keep the top up on the car or I'll end up as red as a lobster." Now it was his turn to fake a smile.

Lydia saw the residue of hurt from the morning's discussion hanging on him like a shroud. His shoulders slumped, his posture loose and lacking energy.

"I shouldn't be long. I'll be back before supper." Wade stood and fished his keys and wallet from the basket on the counter.

He stepped across the kitchen to her. "I love you."

She looked him in the eyes. "I know."

Silence emerged between them. An entire conversation hung unspoken in the air. She wasn't ready to make peace yet, but *damn*. The coldness of her reply even surprised her.

"I love you, too," Lydia said. "Be safe. Supper will be ready at five."

With that, Wade turned and headed out through the back door. She heard the Valiant come to life in the driveway a minute later.

Lydia didn't watch him leave, but from the sounds of the tires mixing it up with the gravel where the driveway met the road, Wade was eager to get where he was going.

Lydia stood in the kitchen for a moment, contemplating her next move. She had chores to do, but she wasn't very motivated to do them. The experience in the garden had done something to her. She felt awakened yet completely run down.

*Maybe the heat took more out of you than you realize*, she thought.

That had to be it. Reading for a while in the cool house would give her a restorative break before she tackled her chores. She searched her memory for her library copy of *A Tale of Two Cities* and remembered last seeing it on the nightstand beside her bed. In her current state, that room felt unreasonably far away. Nevertheless, she made her way across the main floor and up the stairs.

Entering the second-floor hall, she smiled as her eyes took in the sight of Adeline's room. The room seemed to radiate happiness as the sun poured in through the windows. All the pastels, all the soft surfaces, and all that remained of Adeline's life stared back at her. But that didn't feel as heavy as it had just days before. Lydia somehow felt less dreadful, less worried. She knew why; her little girl was here with her. And she always would be.

Lydia continued down the hall to the primary bedroom. As she'd remembered, the book sat on the nightstand beside the bed, patiently waiting for her return. She considered reading there on the bed, but the layer of garden sweat and soil coating her skin and clothes wouldn't allow it. Her chair in the downstairs sitting room was ideal. She was also far less likely to fall asleep reading in her chair than on her bed.

Her mind now fixed on the sitting room, Lydia left her bedroom and headed for the stairs. The book felt unusually heavy in her hands, the hall darker than the midday light should've allowed. Her house shoes pulled on her feet like lead weights.

*You may fall asleep in that chair after all.*

Lydia stopped mid-step as she reached the top of the stairs. Behind her, to the right, the door to the hall bath muffled the sounds of running water.

She slowly turned her head, hoping her eyes would discount the lies her ears surely told. Door shut—no light to be seen under or around it.

*Am I imagining this? Did I climb up on the bed to read and fall asleep?*

As if to distract her from her rambling thoughts, the door eased open on its hinges a few inches.

*Bring it back, Lydia,* the voice said. *I need you here with me, not wandering through possibilities in your room.*

With the door now partially open, the sound of running water in the tub smacked off the hard surfaces of the dark bathroom.

Lydia stood frozen as her mind fought to comprehend what her eyes gathered. Then she moved.

One step.

Then the next.

Into the bathroom.

She reached back and shut the door behind her, entering complete and utter darkness.

---

The total lack of light threw her vision into fits, mixing images and imagination in a swirl of the real and unreal. The mildly sulfuric scent of fresh well water crawled into her sinuses.

She felt her feet on the cold tile floor. She heard the deafening crash of water around her.

Her hands moved to her waist to unbutton her pants. She slowly swayed her hips side-to-side while she pressed down on the waistband. She pressed until they fell into a puddle around her feet. Then she slowly stepped out of them and lifted her shirt over her head.

She removed her undergarments and discarded them to the darkness beside her.

The sound of the water in the tub screamed at her from every corner, every angle, every inch of the room.

Slowly, things became barely visible in a mix of familiar shadows and shapes.

The edge of the tub. The pedestal sink. The toilet. Familiar objects in unfamiliar form.

Calm, composed, and in complete surrender to the forces at play, Lydia lifted one pointed foot.

*I've been here before. In a dream. At her grave.*

Lydia's mind raced. Memories of her experience in the garden earlier that day blitzed her from every direction.

Clouds. Path.

The clawfoot tub. The one above Adeline's grave.

Lydia couldn't tell if her eyes were open or closed, if what she saw was a vision presented by her mind or her eyes.She was in the bathroom. She was in the cemetery.

Foot suspended above water, head lifted, chin up.

As her begrimed toes met the hot water's surface, a whisper so present and so real ripped her mind open.

"Mama."

Lydia shuddered and lowered her foot into the scalding hot water. "Baby, I'm here."

A hand moved up her submerged calf, welcoming her to the water. The water felt on the verge of boiling, then felt frigid. Goosebumps emerged on her legs and across her body.

Lydia committed her weight to the tub. Her back leg entered the water. She turned in place and lowered her body until she came to rest, seated in the tub.

The deluge of water and sound seized. The immediate silence turned to static in her ears.

Lydia looked at the shadows of her knees breaching the water before her like two hulking black islands on the other side of a lightless world, the sea around them empty in all directions.

She guided her hands over the peaks, spreading the water but feeling nothing under hand. Then she lathered the water into onto her skin like a balm, curing the pain, the loss, the cruel, grueling time between happiness and death.

Forms resembling hands spread the viscous fluid over her neck, shoulders, and arms. She leaned into them, accepting their will.

Two children's hands emerged from the black water, slipped up the sides of her neck, and cradled her face. She exhaled everything as the hands pulled her steadily into the water.

She extended her legs, never touching the porcelain sides. The tub seemed boundless before her, a pool of nothing, endless and vast.

She slid completely under.

The darkness accepted her.

"Breathe with me," the voice whispered to her through the water, across all the planes between the living and the dead. "Breathe with me, Mama."

# CHAPTER ELEVEN

Violent forces propelled Lydia from the water. She shot upward into blinding light, water shooting from her in all directions.

"No! No! No!" a familiar voice that wasn't Adeline's said.

Lydia found herself lying on her side on the bathroom floor, her stomach and lungs contracting violently to evacuate the water from her body.

The words, *Breathe, Mama*, echoed in her ears.

Desperation and strength overwhelmed her as she pushed up from the floor. She was on her hands and knees, gasping desperately, each breath of air more necessary than the last.

She looked to her side as she fought for breath and saw Wade seated, his clothes soaked. His eyes were wild, his face flushed red. He had pulled her from the tub, just as they'd pulled Adeline from the same tub only two weeks before.

Reality broke over her like a rogue wave. Wade had saved her from drowning.

*Why didn't he leave me with her?*

The answer was obvious, but the question persisted in her mind. She couldn't think clearly, the drowning waging a battle between her present being and who she'd been on the other side of the light. Lydia was back, but—she wasn't. She felt segmented, partial, torn in half.

The dark and the light.

Wade stood and tried to lift her, but he struggled to grip her wet skin. His feet slid on the slick tiles beneath them.

She slipped into unconsciousness at the sounds of his sobbing.

Lydia came to, still on her side but in the hall now. She lay there alone, naked and trembling. In the distance, she heard a steady but inconsistent banging.

She lifted her head and looked down the hall to the primary bedroom. The door was closed and barely visible in the dark.

*What time is it?*

Her mind spun like a top, tottering about. She looked to her right and saw twilight haunting the windows in Adeline's bedroom.

She strained to think, to pull the scene around her into a clear picture. She grasped at context, contours, and memory.

She'd been in the hall bath. Wade had been there, panicking.

*You were drowning, and he saved you.*

The banging assaulted her ears again. Lydia felt percussions synched with the sound. She looked down the dark hall in search of the origin. This time, her eyes picked up a pattern in the dark. Faint light pulsed around their bedroom door with every emittance of sound.

It became clear someone was banging on the door, which pulsed with every strike.

*Who could that be, and why are they banging on the door?*

It had to be Wade.

*Why doesn't he open the door? Why am I laying naked in the hall while he's in the bedroom?*

Lydia rose to her knees, head down, and caught her breath. Wet coughs wracked her body. She spit indiscriminately to clear her mouth of the water coating her mouth, throat, and lungs.

A groan escaped her as she slowly crawled on her hands and knees down the hall to the door. Her weakness surprised her. She felt as if the day had vacuumed the energy from her body.

Lydia registered Wade's voice between bangs on the door. She heard him gasping for air between rounds of violence.

"Wade—I'm here. What's—happening? What's wrong with the door?"

She collapsed onto her back in front of the door and stared at the ceiling, struggling to breathe. She'd only crawled twenty feet, but she felt like she'd run a hundred miles.

Lydia sensed Wade on the floor on the opposite side of the door. Only three feet separated them, yet he felt out of reach.

"You weren't supposed to be home," she said with a strange sense of finality.

"Lydia? Thank God!"

She'd never heard him so distraught. He sounded like a man on his last breath.

"I was gone the entire afternoon," he said through the door. "I came home and couldn't find you. I searched the whole house. I was on my way back downstairs when I checked the hall bathroom." He paused, grabbing a breath between sobs. "You were drowning, but... what the hell were you doing in the dark like that?"

More breathing.

"I ran in here to call for help, but the phone line is dead," Wade continued. "When I turned to run back to you, the door was shut, and now the doorknob is broken. I tried to open the window to cry for help, but the windows are jammed shut. How is any of this possible?"

With little thought, Lydia asked, "Nothing makes sense, does it?" Wonder filled her.

Realization settled on Lydia like the heaviest matter in the universe. There was a force containing Wade to the room. Everything she'd seen, every experience she'd had with Adeline's spirit was *real*. Adeline was protecting their reunion.

Wade shot back, "Lydia, you need help. You have to open the door. I'm trapped in here. We need to get you to the hospital. Now!"

"No," she replied. "That's not happening."

Silence.

"What?" Wade asked, completely mowed over by her response.

Lydia sat up. She propped her shoulder against the wall, strength returning to her in a flood.

She looked down the hall, eyes focused on the light now emanating from Adeline's bedroom. Just moments before, the hall was completely dark.

"Lydia! Open the door!"

She ignored him, eyes locked on the wet footprints at the end of the hall. Her eyes tracked them from the hall bathroom to the landing.

*She's waiting for me*, Lydia thought. She leaned onto the wall for balance as she came to her feet.

She turned, gently placed a hand against the door, and said with genuine compassion, "I love you, Wade."

Lydia turned and walked down the hall on unsteady legs as Wade threw himself against the door behind her.

# CHAPTER TWELVE

Lydia walked in lockstep beside the wet footprints on the back porch. The steps ended where the bottom porch step met the yard. There, Lydia stood naked under the light of a waxing crescent moon, her rebirth imminent.

She closed her eyes and whispered, "Hello, dearest Adeline."

"Hello, Mama."

When Lydia opened her eyes again, Adeline stood there, naked and soaking wet—a younger mirror reflection of her mother. Lydia could hardly breathe.

Adeline appeared as she'd looked the day she died—vibrant, loving, and pure. There were no blemishes, wrinkles, or scars with which to ponder. Death had not changed her. Lydia marveled that death had preserved her perfectly. Perhaps the preservation of a soul was an underappreciated blessing of death. While the body lay discarded to the pressures of time and earth, the soul passed into perfect preservation, an eternal gift granted to those without life.

Adeline reached out and took her mother's hand. Then, without a word, she led Lydia across the backyard, beneath the shadow of the clothesline.

Adeline walked with her right hand passing through the garments until she stopped before the dress Lydia had donned to her funeral.

Lydia smiled and plucked the dress from the line with care. She gathered the dress in her hands before slipping it over her head. She did so methodically, honoring the weight and significance of the moment.

When she finished adjusting her dress, she looked at Adeline, now clothed in her burial gown. The simple, yet elegant, white dress glowed subtly against the summer night.

They continued, their bare feet absorbing the lingering day's heat from the warm grass. Reaching the midpoint between the house and the path to the cemetery, Lydia paused to take in her surroundings.

Thirty yards behind her and nearly level with the treetops across the yard, Wade raged against their bedroom window. His voice had almost given out as he desperately called for her. The absence of light in his room made him appear as a ghost pressed against glass, distant and manic. Although she couldn't hear him, she imagined the utter helplessness in his cries. She suppressed a sudden realization that she had turned her back on the man she'd loved for so many years. However, it was easy to bury the emotion under the mass of a mother's love. She blocked out the sounds of his unraveling, as she turned from him and followed Adeline to the path in the woods.

Lydia's surroundings along the path to the cemetery came alive with their every step. Each footfall brought new life to the darkness between the towering trees. Shadows darted among the trunks, whipping the ferns into a dancing mass carpeting the forest floor. Some resembled birds of flight, others bore the traits of four-legged creatures, eyes alight in the night's energy.

Adeline led the way down the path, occasionally stealing a glance over her shoulder at her mother. Lydia's heart fluttered with each look.

She couldn't take her eyes off Adeline. Her curls bounced in unison with her steps, expanding and contracting in a consistent back and forth with gravity.

They entered the clearing of the cemetery, still in silence. Lydia felt a vibration in her core, a sense of homecoming. She'd always found the family cemetery to be a comforting refuge, a place to escape the world and bend the ears of those who passed before her. Before tonight, she'd had plenty of discussions with the dead, but never had they responded, let alone come to life like Adeline had.

Adeline stopped at the foot of a fresh mound of dirt. In the strange light of the evening, Adeline's plot stood in stark contrast to the aged plots of their kin. Lydia's nose filled with the smell of freshly disturbed clay and the surrounding pines.

Adeline took her hand again and slowly guided Lydia to her knees in the soil above the girl's grave. Lydia wondered if she could believe her eyes. If Adeline was truly here with her, above the earth, her resurrection was that of biblical magnitude. She had risen from the dead, guiding her disciple to her knees in the dirt above her previous resting place.

The girls sat on their heels, knees nearly touching.

Adeline leaned forward with shimmering eyes. "Hello, Mama." She giggled lightly at the fun of the welcome.

"Hello, Adeline. I can't believe you came back to see me. I am lost without you, little one." Tears of joy and grief collected in her eyes. "I'm so sorry, baby. I'm just so emotional. I've been a complete mess since you left us. And now, you're here. I'm with you..." She inhaled deeply and exhaled, rolling her eyes upward to control her emotions. "This is crazy." She laughed nervously, her face twisting into a cry.

Adeline took her mother's hands in hers. The girl's hands were soft and warm, the very hands Lydia would kiss each night before putting the girl to bed. Lydia lifted one of them to her cheek, sweeping it back and forth.

Adeline smiled. "Now, Mama, please don't cry. I'm here now. You haven't lost me. No more tears."

With that, Adeline brought their hands from her lap to the dirt beside their knees. She pressed Lydia's hands into the soil, then used them to pull dirt to the side, removing a small layer of grave filler.

"I understand," Lydia whispered, her face slack in the moonlight.

Adeline smiled again, her satisfaction evident. The girl began digging with her hands. Lydia joined her.

Time looped with every handful of soil Lydia removed from her daughter's grave.

She kept her eyes down, focused on her work, pacing herself and never flagging. She felt Adeline working quietly at her side.

Lydia had no concern for the moist clay staining her dress or for her aching hands and broken nails. None of that mattered. She dug, then she dug more, an endless cycle.

The moon journeyed across the night sky as they worked, no one around to disturb them. Stars charged the dome above them. The shadows in the trees moved with feral anticipation.

Lydia never tired, cramped, or became winded. An unrelenting force powered her until her fingers struck the hard surface of Adeline's casket.

Lydia paused, crouching over her work. Awareness touched her again for the first time since the digging had started. Her eyes darted around the cavernous hole now cradling her. Adeline had slipped away from her amid the trance. Panic threatened to replace the blind energy orchestrating her actions.

Lydia closed her eyes tight, repressing a wave of nausea. The musty, sharp smell of clay overpowered her.

She assured herself.

*She's here. She's here. She's here.*

A soft tapping from beneath her fingers stole her panic.

"I'm here," Lydia said.

Adeline's voice penetrated the casket on which Lydia perched. "Come lay with me, Mama."

Lydia's arms shook as relief and joy blanketed her heart. She bent forward, kissed the coffin lid. "I'm coming, sweetheart."

She cleared the loose soil from the foot of the casket behind her and made a sweeping round of the remaining surface. Lydia found the seam of the casket's lid along its left edge and pried steadily with her hardening hands. It wouldn't budge.

Suddenly, the lid's seal gave way, and her fingers slipped into the gap between the lid and base. Cool air beneath the lid kissed her fingertips. She adjusted her position beside the coffin, drew a wet, calculated breath, and lifted.

There, head on pillow, arms crossed on her chest, lay Adeline. She was beautiful in the soft moonlight. The shadows hid the details of her demise.

Lydia's reality disintegrated at the sight of her dead daughter. The roof over her heart collapsed under the stress of her grief, love, and anxiety. She moaned as she pulled at her bosom. The stars above rained down from the sky, as the trees bowed and groaned.

Lydia crawled into the casket, took one final look at the world collapsing around them, and lowered the lid.

The casket harbored an impenetrable darkness, the world outside silenced by the insulated lid. However, Lydia felt rolling thunder threaten the outside world as a summer storm coalesced somewhere out of reach.

She nestled her face into Adeline's cold neckline. She whispered into the cramped expanse. "I'll see you in our dreams tonight, little one. Adventures await us on the other side. You and me, we'll dance with the moon and kiss the clouds. The dark doesn't stand a chance against us." She laid her hand on Adeline's.

Lydia upheld her side of the exchange, but Adeline remained silent. Lydia wondered if she'd ever hear Adeline's voice again. She shrugged the concern away, confident anything was possible where Adeline took her.

Above them, thick raindrops struck the coffin lid. Lydia heard pebbles and loose soil tumble to the lid from the angled walls of the grave under the influence of the building rain and wind.

As Lydia drifted into asphyxiation, she saw movement in the darkness of the casket. In her final moment of consciousness, Lydia smiled as Adeline opened her eyes to the dark.

# QUICK FAVOR

Thank you so much for dedicating your time to reading this book! May I ask a quick favor?

Will you please take a moment to leave a review on Amazon, Goodreads, or wherever you purchased the book? Your words have power. Your review can help this book serve more people. I appreciate you!

# WHAT'S NEXT?

*Bury the Child* is a prequel to The Haunting of the Whispering House series. Book 1 of the series, *Burn the Girls*, becomes available in the fall of 2023.

Visit https://www.lucasmarinowrites.com/ for the latest updates.

Subscribe to Lucas's Substack, Time Stands Still, for serial fiction, reflections on books and music, and other ramblings. https://lucasmarinofiction.substack.com/

# THOUGHTS AND THANKS

This book would have been impossible without the support and feedback from my wife, Tammie. She played an integral role in vetting my plot, hashing out character traits, and serving as resident motherhood expert. Although she demands cover credit and unrealistic financial compensation, she'll have to settle for marriage, three kids, and a steady role as my advisor for the remaining books in the series.

Our kids, Madelyn, Gabriel, and Caleb, also contributed to this book's success. Madelyn, my youngest fan of creepy things, was the first human to read the final three chapters of this story. We sat on the couch at 1 a.m. on a summer night, parent and child, reading the reunion of Lydia and Adeline in silence. Her smile at the end confirmed the story contained the appropriate level of creepiness to satisfy the harshly critical mind of a twelve-year-old girl. I'm grateful for that moment together and Madelyn's approval.

It should come as no surprise that Tammie and Madelyn inspired my depictions of Lydia and Adeline. Their mannerisms, conversations, and relationship informed my blueprints for Lydia and Adeline. In fact, when I completed the first draft, I realized I'd misspelled Adeline's name as "Adelyn" for the entire latter half of the book. That's just one minor example of how the real thing influenced my writing when I was most vulnerable.

Our boys, Caleb and Gabriel, provided positivity and technical support in spades. Gabriel listened to me rant about character conflict, wild plot twists, and the joys of self-publishing during our Saturday night hangouts. Caleb provided the most advanced home network this side of James City County, VA. Without his genius and persistent troubleshooting and corrective maintenance, I would have written this book on the other side of town via a cellular hotspot. Thanks, dude!

My desire to write fiction, particularly the suspenseful kind, started early in life. Dad spent much of my youth working several jobs around military deployments at sea. That left Mom to raise two knucklehead boys and put herself through college. As you can see, hard work is a part of our landscape. Art can sometimes get lost in that shuffle. Mom made sure I had the latest Stephen King novel in my hands, and Dad provided the music. I distinctly recall sitting in my small room in 1990, reading my *Four Past Midnight* paperback to Metallica's *...And Justice for All.*

If I wasn't reading, I would play the guitar. I aspired to become a professional writer or musician. Years later, I chased music with my parents' encouragement. How cool is that? After a few years, I abandoned that pursuit and joined the Coast Guard. Now, 25 years later, I'm finally committed to life as a writer, and again, my parents encourage me. Mom, Dad, I love you!

The list of professionals who supported this novella starts with my friend, book coach, and editor, Zach Bohannon. Simply put, Zach made this book better. He is an accomplished writer and a tremendous coach. I encourage every writer to find their Zach and never let them go. You're stuck with me now, dude.

Clarrisa Yeo is the talent behind the amazing book cover. Clarrisa, you knocked it out of the park! Thank you so much for making such a significant contribution to this project.

Jen Piceno, thank you for proofreading the book! Your energy and enthusiasm for this work warms me.

To my mentor and dear friend, Honorée Corder, thank you for the encouragement, accountability, and publishing guidance. Our morning conversations kept me focused and confident. Thank you!

Finally, I extend my sincere thanks to the early- release readers on Substack. I initially released this novella as a weekly Substack serial in its unedited form. You braved an unchecked world, shared it with friends, and motivated me. I look forward to sharing the next serial story with you starting—now!

# ABOUT THE AUTHOR

Lucas writes thriller, suspense, and horror fiction. If he's not writing, he's reading, playing guitar, or enjoying time with his family. Lucas is also the host of *The Suspense is Killing Me* podcast.

A military engineer by experience, he spent twenty-one years in the United States Coast Guard. He earned his Doctor of Engineering and Master of Science degrees in Engineering Management and Systems Engineering at The George Washington University.

He now lives in a pile of trees in Virginia.